The Fall

Marga
Minco

The Fall

TRANSLATED FROM THE DUTCH BY
Jeannette Kalker Ringold

PETER OWEN · LONDON

ISBN 0 7206 0789 2

Translated from the Dutch *De Val*

PETER OWEN PUBLISHERS
73 Kenway Road London SW5 ORE

First published in Great Britain 1990
© Marga Minco 1983
English translation © Jeannette Kalker Ringold 1990

Printed in Great Britain by Billings of Worcester

I imagine, sometimes, that if a film could be made of one's life, every other frame would be death. It goes so fast we're not aware of it. Destruction and resurrection in alternate beats of being, but speed makes it seem continuous. But you see, kid, with ordinary consciousness you can't even begin to know what's happening.

Saul Bellow *The Dean's December*

Introduction

'UNDERSTATEMENT' is the term most often used by critics to describe Marga Minco's style. Restrained emotion is her hallmark, and this is particularly important when we realize that the subject of most of her work is the Second World War and its aftermath. She writes from her experience, but her work is not strictly autobiographical. Minco thinks that prose writers can never be restrained enough, that a work can only gain by elimination of all that is superfluous, all 'decoration'. Above all, she wants to let the facts speak: 'If you report them in the right way, they should be able to do the work. You also have to leave something for the reader. You should choose between facts and feelings. . . . Feelings are important, but you must be careful with them, you can kill facts with them' (from the introduction to *Het huis hiernaast* (*The House Next Door*), Amsterdam, 1965).

Marga Minco was born Sara Menco in March 1920 in a small town which was later annexed to Breda, a city in the south of Holland. She was the youngest of three children in an orthodox Jewish family. After high school, she became an apprentice reporter for the *Bredasche Courant*. Because of pressure from the local Nazi leader, she was forced to leave this job the day after the German invasion of Holland in 1940. Shortly afterwards, she contracted a form of tuberculosis which necessitated a long stay in a hospital and then in a sanatorium. After she recuperated, the only work the Nazis would allow her to do was inside the Jewish community. She gave drawing lessons at a Jewish school until most of the children had been deported.

Minco's sister Bettie and her husband were deported in 1942 during one of the first Nazi raids in Amsterdam. Her parents, who like all Dutch Jews over fifty had been forced to move to Amsterdam, were deported in 1943. In that same year her brother Dave and his wife were also caught and deported. Marga herself was able to escape and went into hiding, first with a very poor day-labourer's family and later with a potter in a small town near Haarlem where several other young writers and artists were also hiding. In 1944, Minco and some of these artists went to live in an unoccupied house near the centre of Amsterdam where they spent the rest of the war. With her false identification and her bleached hair she was able to survive the war. None of her immediate family returned. In August 1945 she married the poet and Shakespeare translator Bert Voeten. They have two daughters and still live in Amsterdam.

During the first decade after the war, Marga Minco contributed short stories to several newspapers and journals. In 1957 *Het bittere kruid* (*Bitter Herbs*) was published. In this 'small chronicle' the narrator, a girl much younger than Minco was at that time, tells the story of a Jewish family in the Second World War. The book became a best-seller and was translated into at least eight languages. It has made Minco one of the most-read Dutch authors of the post-war years. In 1958 she received the Vijverberg prize of the Jan Campert Foundation for this novel. The short story 'Het adres' ('The Address') was also published in 1957 and was honoured with the Mutator Prize. Minco's second book, a collection of short stories entitled *De andere Kant* (*The Other Side*), appeared in 1959 and in 1966 came *Een leeg huis* (*An Empty House*, published in English by Peter Owen, 1990). More complex in structure than her previous work, this novel tells the story of two young women and takes place during the aftermath of the war, in the years 1945 to 1950. Marga Minco's work also includes some humorous stories, as well as a children's book and several television plays. Her most recent novel is *De glazen brug*, published in English as *The Glass*

Bridge (Peter Owen, 1988). This was commissioned as a gift book for the 1986 Dutch Bookweek and, like *An Empty House*, is set just after the Second World War. Once again, its theme is the need to discover the truth about the past so that more sense can be made of the present.

First published in 1983, *De Val* (*The Fall*) covers the events of only two days, the day of the accident and the day after. Yet Minco has again woven together the events of the present and of the past in a most complex way. The origin of the novel was a newspaper story about a similar accident (in the town in question the municipal heating system has since been changed because of it). The story starts out as the report of the accident, but the several meanings of the Dutch title indicate that it will be more complex than this. We discover that facts are never as simple as they appear, and that trying to figure out the truth about the past is a very uncertain affair.

There are at least four significant meanings of the Dutch word *val*. First of all, it refers to a physical descent, such as when Frieda trips on the staircase and is left behind, and also her accident at the end of the story. Secondly there is the meaning of *val* as 'trap', such as that into which the family *falls* when caught by the Nazis. Thirdly, there is the meaning of *val* as 'downfall'. And fourthly is the meaning which indicates the importance of chance, the fact that everything depends on coincidence, as in the Dutch expression *naar de val gaat het af*. (The word for coincidence in Dutch is *toeval*.)*

Even though Marga Minco's most important and most moving stories are gathered from her experience as a Jew in the Netherlands during the Second World War, the beauty of her work, and the universality of its dominant themes – alienation and loneliness – are such that new translations are still appearing in languages as diverse as Welsh, Bulgarian and Hebrew.

Jeannette Kalker Ringold

January 1990

---

* I am indebted for this fourth definition to Wim Sanders's review of *The Wall*, published in *Het Parool*, 18 May 1983.

*I*T HAS BEEN established that the two municipal mechanics on that Thursday morning did not go as usual straight from the central boiler house to their work, but stopped first at the Salamander. At night there had been a heavy frost, the mercury had dropped to ten degrees below zero and ice started forming at once on the fogged windows of their Volkswagen bus. It is possible that they thought it was too cold or too dark for the job they had to do; it is also possible that it was because of the reaction of Baltus who was behind the wheel and braked automatically when, in passing the café, he saw the fluorescent lights flash on above the bar.

'Who do we have here so bright and early!' Carla looked surprised as the two men stepped inside, stamping and rubbing their hands. Immediately after she had turned on the light, she plugged in the coffee-machine, more for herself than because she expected customers that early – it was just past seven-thirty.

Silently the visitors pulled off their jackets, sat down at the table next to the juke-box and placed their packets of cigarette tobacco in front of them.

'The usual, I suppose?' Carla had pushed the cups under the machine and stood waiting for the bubbling and hissing of the boiling water to stop. 'Are you starting work or did you do the night-shift?'

'We don't do the night-shift,' said Baltus. He sounded surly.

'Oh, I was just wondering.' She felt that they were not yet approachable and therefore she decided not to comment on the cold. Besides, she would have to say the same sort of thing over and over again during the day.

Bent over the small table, their heads almost touching, they drank the hot coffee without blowing, each waiting, it seemed, for the other to open his mouth first. In the cold fluorescent light which furrowed their features, they took on a conspiratorial air. Not until they had finished their second cup and rolled their first cigarette did Baltus break the silence, in which only the clicking of spoons and clacking of the central heating could be heard.

'To think they let him go on all that time, I can't believe it.'

'Sooner or later you get caught, you can see that.'

'Did you know it would happen?'

'Not me. It's not my area.' Verstrijen edged his chair aside and looked sideways up at Carla who, behind the counter, was taking a bite from a cheese roll.

Baltus leant with his elbows on the table, the broad head on the short neck tucked between his shoulders. With his stocky figure he had the look of a weight-lifter, and in fact he had shown he had the strength of one when he moved the juke-box as if it were a folding chair. Verstrijen was younger, a man in his mid-thirties with alert, grey-blue eyes, dark-blond, curly hair and a carefully trimmed moustache. He reminded Carla of her gym teacher in elementary school. They were steady customers, who usually came by about four times a week, though never as early as this.

Later she remembered that they had really only talked about the construction scandal which all the local newspapers were full of. She had heard Baltus say that he knew the subcontractor who had swindled the lot out of more than a million, and that he had never trusted him. After that they fell silent again, sat stiff and dour facing each other, and rolled another cigarette. Baltus drummed on the formica with his heavy fingers; Verstrijen stared mainly at the wall – for the rest of the day it would be best to leave him alone, Carla could tell from his back. Neither one of them made any sign of leaving.

While she was wiping the tray around the coffee-machine with a cloth, Carla asked if by chance they had a difficult job ahead of them, but even that direct question did not get a direct answer.

'Same again today,' said Verstrijen. 'We have that job as long as the water-level is high.' Baltus pulled vigorously on his cigarette, exhaling the smoke as though he were blowing steam. They stood up a few minutes before eight. The reluctance with which they pushed back their chairs was apparent in all their movements, the way in which they stretched their legs, shoved themselves into their jackets, pulled on their gloves.

'Well, let's get a move on,' said Baltus.

Carla hid her annoyance with difficulty. They shouldn't come and spoil her day so early in the morning. To her question whether they would as usual on Thursday come by again at five o'clock, she received no answer, for at that moment a messenger boy stepped inside. He was wearing a black leather coat, and a woollen scarf wound three times around his neck made the head under the black moped helmet seem even smaller than it was.

'Where do you have to go?' he asked, blowing on his hands.

'To Uiterwaarden Street,' said Baltus. 'Would you like a lift?'

'I wouldn't mind. I'm freezing on that thing. Do you have a lot of work there?'

'It all depends,' said Verstrijen.

'I have to be in the area. I'll come and have a look.'

'You can come and warm your hands, son. And how!' Baltus walked wide-legged to the door.

Verstrijen hesitated a moment, turned quickly towards Carla, raised his hand and winked at her before going outside.

By the time that they were once more in the bus, half an hour had passed. Baltus turned on the headlights and looked at the thin, glistening precipitation on the asphalt. The streets were still dark, but above the square ahead of them the sky was beginning to lighten very slowly as though the day had as much trouble getting started as they had.

*F*RIEDA BORGSTEIN was awakened at seven-thirty. Usually she stayed in bed, but this morning it cost her no effort to deviate from this habit. Although she hadn't slept too well – the second sleeping-pill had not helped until the latter part of the night – she was immediately wide awake.

She looked forward to the day ahead of her, in which for once she had all sorts of things to do, and stepped with one movement into her ready slippers, much too fast; she had to grab on to the chair next to her bed. In the lower part of her back she felt a violent stab of pain, and in her heel muscles a cramp that climbed up to her calves and the back of her knees, which made standing impossible. She fell back on the bed and began massaging her legs. These last years especially she was assailed by pains from the moment she got up. It made her angry that they never failed to come. She could not accept the arbitrary control of her body; she kept hoping that once again, even if only once, she could feel as she had before. As before – what had that been like? Hunched, her hands around her ankles, she searched for an answer. But nothing came to mind, so she gave up. It was now more important to her to get up again, cautiously.

'Come on,' she muttered, while she carefully stretched her back. 'Pain means that you exist.' She stuck her legs out, moved her feet back and forth, let them drop and again got into her slippers. The cramp eased. Still bent, on guard against another attack, she shuffled to the bathroom, supporting herself by chair-back, wall, doorknob and sink. She switched on the light above the mirror, let water run into a glass and took a good gulp. Drops trickled from the corners of her mouth. She wiped them off with the back of her hand and nodded at her image, as every morning. She wished herself good morning because there was no one else. Not until after she had washed her hands and face did she take off her night-dress, and now she stood in her flannel underwear, her arms and legs disconcertingly thin and shrivelled. She looked at herself as if it were the first time she had seen herself like that and quickly grabbed a dress which hung within reach on the door.

When Gerrie brought breakfast, she first came

to your bed. If she didn't find you there, she would peek around the corner into the bathroom and would catch you. In her hurry to prevent this, Frieda put her dress on back to front, took it off with grim tugging, turned it around and again stuck her hands into the sleeves. After that, breathing hard, she worked her head through the neck opening.

Tomorrow she would take a shower.

Tomorrow she would dress up.

Tomorrow she would go to the hairdresser.

Today, preparations would have to be made.

In front of the sink she completed her toilet with a couple of cursory passes of the comb through her dry curls and a whisk of the powder-puff over her face. Reddish brown bits of fluff remained on her cheek-bones and in her eyebrows. She brushed them away, smudged her cheeks, used the puff once more and shuffled back to the living-room bedroom, where she pushed open the curtains and went to sit near the window to consult the notes she had made the night before.

It was still dark. In the window she could see only the reflection of the room and that of herself under the lamp. But above the office buildings across the street the ash-coloured light began to flow and take on hues, from drab yellow to pale blue.

She liked the shrinking darkness, the rising light over the city. When she felt well, she followed the break of day from her fourth-floor window, even though the new buildings did block some of her view. She would have preferred it if houses could have been built on that open terrain, houses with front- and backyards, so that she could have watched the lives of families, of people who eventually would have become familiar to her. The civil servants who, winter and summer, sat under the same glaring yellow ceiling light behind their steel-framed windows, seemed remote from her. They were moving dolls who all looked the same.

The separation between the greyness of the sky and the roofs became wider, and behind the low houses further down the street there emerged in that opening TV aerials, treetops and a church spire. She thought of all those mornings on which, immediately after getting up, they had looked out from their bedroom window over the river and its banks looming from the mist. Jacob murmured behind her: 'The water is different every day.' And then she said: 'You always say that.' And he: 'But it is.' Meaningless phrases, but through repetition they came to have the significance of a formula, part of the ritual with which they started their day together.

Smiling, she put the notepad in front of her, and she was just pulling off the cap of her fountain-pen when there was knocking at the door. Gerrie came in with her breakfast.

'Good morning, Mrs Borgstein. What do we have there? You're sitting up already?' The girl called out with the same indestructible cheerfulness she displayed when she found her still in bed. 'What do we have there, Mrs Borgstein? Still in bed? No desire to get up? And it's going to be such a beautiful day.' Talk normally, Frieda would then want to say, we don't need encouragement any more, we can decide for ourselves whether we feel like it or not. Do you think perhaps that we've always been like this and that old age is an inborn disability? She would have to let that out some time, but today she would keep it to herself; today she would not be annoyed at anything, nothing must stand in the way of her plans. She smiled at the girl who had a markedly turned-up nose, accentuated by her very short upper lip, which made her look as though she were continually gasping for breath.

'It was down to ten degrees below zero last night,' said Gerrie. She had put the tray on the table and walked back to the door. 'There's a freezing wind and we'll get a snowfall as well.'

'Oh come on, it doesn't look like that at all. Look at the sky.' The smile did not leave Frieda's face.

'It was just on the news. And they said that the freezing spell will persist for some time.' The girl had half turned away. Frieda saw the enlarged silhouette of her bouncy profile outlined against

24

the light-grey panel. Just like one of the shadow animals that Jacob would magically create on the wall for the children. He was very good at it, his hands made whatever the children demanded.

'I have so many severe winters behind me already. I'll get through this one as well.' She waved her hand to indicate that the subject didn't please her, and at the same time she saw a park in winter, frozen ponds swarming with skaters, among them Jacob with the children behind him, waving to her when they passed by. She waved back, tried to follow their white hats in the crowd as long as possible.

'No one is going out today, Mrs Borgstein. Just stay comfortably indoors,' said Gerrie before closing the door behind her.

Frieda looked at her hand which was limply moving back and forth at the wrist. The movement surprised her. She took the teapot, poured some tea and slowly began to butter her bread. It wasn't until she had cut it into squares that she discovered she hadn't taken any cheese. Busy with the transparent, stuck-together cheese slices, she smelt the fragrance of fresh bread and fried eggs. The sun shone through the kitchen window and threw light spots on the red and white chequered tablecloth. They were all talking: Leo and Olga about school, Jacob about the office – he had a busy day but would try to be home on time. She closed her eyes for a moment to bring them closer to her, laid down her knife, pushed her plate away, leant back.

The four of them were standing at the bottom of the stairs. Her hand clasped Olga's cold fingers. Leo said he'd be curious, he'd have to see it first. Jacob reassured him, it had all been arranged. Nervously she went over what she might have forgotten. It might be years before they could return. The heater was still burning, but the fire would go out by itself. Hein had said that they should leave the curtains drawn apart; that would arouse the least suspicion. In the dark, the whole house already felt deserted.

Her gaze now rested on the cabinet facing her, on the portraits in silver frames. Even without these photographs she would always see them in front of her without any effort. As long as she lived, as long as her memory remained intact, she kept them present; with that she justified her existence. She had already managed to reach eighty-five and, who knows, she might get as far as her grandmother who, despite a series of imagined complaints to which she, according to her own predictions, should have succumbed at an early age, had reached ninety-six. At the head of a Friday evening table covered with a damask cloth, surrounded by all her descendants, Moetje, as she was called, slowly placed her hands in her lap, looked over the scene to see whether anything was missing, nodded and breathed her last.

The last time Frieda had sat at such a table was forty years ago. She was celebrating her birthday in a room full of people who had no idea that this was the last time they would be together. How often had she stood afterwards on the threshold of that room in which they had remained young for ever. This picture was enough for her, and year in year out she had let the day pass in silence. Not until now did she think that the age she had reached should be celebrated. The director had agreed with her when she brought it up. 'Of course, Mrs Borgstein. You should do something about it. And we shall too.'

With her forehead almost against the window she looked down. The street lights were still on, although the sun had already cast a thin copper glow over the roofs of the low houses. An official city car drove up, made a sharp turn and stopped across the street. She put on her glasses, pulled the notepad towards her and began calculating. Next to the notes which she had already made she filled in amounts, then added them up to see roughly what she would have to spend. Her passion for making calculations had never left her. When asked why she did it, she said that it kept her mind limber. This time too she did not content herself with balancing her shopping list. Multiplication, long division, even equations developed – a forest of numbers in which she lost herself.

Baltus had parked the Volkswagen bus on the left side of the street, on the pavement right behind the Social Services building, the left front wheel at half a metre from the hot-water vault positioned there. Verstrijen threw the back doors open. Together they carried out the pump fittings, hoses and folding safety gates.

The clock of the church behind the Home sounded the half-hour. Eight-thirty, Verstrijen set his watch, which he had forgotten to wind that morning. 'Yes, reset it,' said Baltus. He stamped vigorously a few times and, crossing his arms, slapped his sides. His clouds of breath looked like those of a horse.

9:40   *11 o'clock*

AT TWENTY to ten the telephone rang in the
director's office, a spacious ground-floor room
with a large window facing the street. The secretary
of the architect, De Vlonder, informed them that
the gentlemen who were going to inspect the Home
at eleven-thirty could be expected half an hour
earlier because of their changed plans. Rena van
Straten, annoyed by this invasion of her daily
schedule, immediately called the kitchen to ask
them to send Bien Hijmans to her.

The head of the household, a robust woman
with sandy, curly hair, a round face and reddish
purple hands, sat down on the edge of her chair,
ready to run away. 'We are very busy in the
reception-room.' She didn't understand why Rena
had called her from her work for a message which
she could just as well have given her on the
telephone. 'That half-hour makes no difference to
us.'

'I don't like an appointment being changed at such short notice. We had planned the affair exactly.' A sharp tap of the pen on the blotting-paper.

'Well, things will work out all right.'

'Didn't you want to let them eat half an hour later?'

'That's what we decided.'

'Now you can keep the regular mealtime.'

'But they're all geared up for the change. Couldn't we leave things as they are?'

'No, I think it would be better if the day took its usual course.'

'Then it will still be rush work for us.'

'It's still early, Bien.'

The director lifted her carefully shaped eyebrows and took a letter from the letter-holder in front of her, an accessory which was part of a geometric pattern, as was everything on the desk. With her sense of order and equanimity she was the direct opposite of the casual, spontaneous Hijmans whose outbursts of temper did from time to time cause commotions. Both radiated a remarkable vitality. Daily association with the aged seemed to enhance it.

Bien pressed her hands together. At any rate it's still too early for fighting, she thought, and she said: 'There's been no lack of interest in us lately. This time even from Sweden.'

'Yes, for the first time. We are making a name

for ourselves.' Rena van Straten smiled. The Home was known not only for its advanced architecture, but the manner in which it was run was also drawing attention, and she was very conscious of her contribution to that aspect.

'Is the architect also coming again?'

'Our own De Vlonder, certainly. He's touring various Homes with the two Swedes. It has gradually become his speciality.'

'He knows what's good for the old folks.'

'And we don't?' It sounded like a reprimand, which she quickly covered by quoting from the letter: '"Architect Langdren will be accompanied by Dr Enquist, the gerontologist from Göteborg". And of course there is also a busybody from the provincial department for care of the aged.'

'Rietmeier.'

'No, someone else is coming in his place.'

'We'll see.' Hijmans had stood up.

'I'll check everything again just before eleven. On the tour I'll save the two-person apartments until the end. After all, those are our pride.' Again, that same self-satisfied smile around the thin lips. 'And I did have something else.'

'Oh really?' Already at the door, Bien turned brusquely. She barely managed to hold back a 'Now what?'

'Mrs Borgstein came to see me this week. She will be eighty-five tomorrow, and she definitely wants to celebrate this birthday.'

'So suddenly? Well, then we'll make a nice day of it.'

'She has all sorts of things in her head. She wants to treat everyone, to place a gigantic order at the bakery. I couldn't talk her out of it.'

'Once Borgstein gets something in her head – well, you know.'

'Don't forget to ask her what she wants to eat.'

'I will.' Now she felt really piqued. She hardly needed such things pointed out to her, they were her speciality. But it pleased her that Borgstein finally wanted to make something of her birthday. She was vigorous and quite with-it, although in her stubbornness of wanting to arrange everything herself she might overdo things. 'As long as it all doesn't become too much for her.'

'What makes you think that? She won't mind the visit. No one will.'

'No, but in spite of themselves . . .'

'The old people can stand a lot, Bien, especially Mrs Borgstein.'

'You never know.' She didn't know why she had said that. She would have liked to touch wood immediately, the unpainted wood under Rena's desk, but she thought it would be too silly to walk back to do so and left the office.

Rena van Straten had brushed aside Hijmans's last remark. Everything was going well, despite the severe winter. No one had become seriously ill, and they hadn't had a death in months. The

visitors would be able to see a classic example of progressive care for the aged. Decisively she picked up a stack of files from her desk, took them to the filing cabinet which stood next to the window. In so doing she caught a glimpse of a grey car, around which two men were engaged in some sort of task.

*W*HILE Bien Hijmans was informing the staff of the earlier than expected visit, Frieda Borgstein was standing in front of her clothes cupboard, from which she extracted a dress she had completely forgotten about, a black one with a light-blue flower print. She couldn't remember how often she had worn the dress, but she did know that she had worn it for the farewell party of the Oosterveens, with whom she had been in hiding. Their emigration to Australia signified the loss of friends who had continued supporting her. They had pressed her almost to come with them, and in their letters they repeated their attempts to persuade her. 'Why don't you come to us, Frieda,' they wrote. 'Start afresh like us?' But she didn't want that. Her place was here. In this city.

The first year of her marriage she had helped Jacob, who at that time had just started his brokerage office, with keeping the books. As the business grew, more trained staff came, the children were born and she involved herself totally with her family.

After the war she had taken bookkeeping courses. She had mastered the subject quickly and accepted a job at a large business office. Her number mania dated from that time. More often than not she took the books home and continued working on them until deep into the night. Her diligence became fanaticism. She found satisfaction in the most difficult calculations and wished to concentrate on nothing else. Numbers were neutral, cold, unemotional; they offered her something to hang on to and screened her from images she could not yet face.

With trembling hands she draped the dress around herself in front of the mirror. Would it still fit? Jacob thought that black looked good on her, even though he preferred to see her in pastels. Once he had brought her a beige silk blouse from Brussels, trimmed with lace and small pearls. 'A treasure,' she cried out. 'It becomes a treasure because you wear it,' he had said. She turned round and looked at him. Without taking her eyes off him she walked with the dress, which undulated with each step as though there were no body behind it, to the cabinet. When she picked up his photograph, she had already forgotten the garment. It fell in a heap in front of her feet.

'How are things now, Jacob?'

'I have made a final arrangement with Hein. He can take us to Switzerland.'

'What does he want for that?'

'A lot of money.'

'How much?'

'Six thousand guilders.'

'But how will you manage that? Now that the business has been placed under Nazi control, you can't get a penny from it. And won't we also need money over there?'

'I've got something in reserve – you know that. But we'll certainly have to sell the family heirlooms and the silverware.'

'Do you think it will work?'

'It has to work, Frieda. Before long the regulations will become even stricter. Then we'll be stuck. We must leave now.'

'Is that boy trustworthy?'

'Hein? I would put my hand in the fire for him. Just as solid as his father. He knows all about the escape route. We are not the first ones he has helped.'

His broad forehead, the wavy hair, the mouth whose left corner would lift slightly, the eyes with the points of light, even the faces of the children and the other family members were dull and grey, and it suddenly cost her an effort to imagine the colours which were lacking. Perhaps colour was the first thing that disappeared at the end of your life, and before closing your eyes you saw nothing but a series of blurred black and white exposures.

With difficulty she bent down to pick up the dress. Undecided, she stood holding it in her hand. Why should she hurry? What difference had it made?

Two hours before curfew Hein came to tell them that they should be standing ready in the hall in half an hour with as little luggage as possible, only the absolute essentials. Once in Switzerland everything would be taken care of. They would first arrive at a reception centre. He had the false papers with him. After his departure they hurriedly took some of their belongings out of their bags and stuffed in other things in their place, running through the house to see if there was anything else they should take along. Leo chose a book; Olga, a summer blouse; Jacob, his travel alarm-clock, which she thought rather ridiculous. 'You do know where we are going?' Well within the half-hour she ran downstairs with the children. Jacob followed them at his leisure and urged them to be calm.

'We won't get far today,' said Leo, who remained sceptical about the success of the undertaking.

'He will take us first to an address outside the city. From there we will move on early tomorrow morning.'

It was a chilly, rainy April evening. She was aware that Olga, who had caught a cold, stood shivering.

'Aren't you wearing your heavy sweater?'

'I couldn't find it in the rush.'

'Wait here, I'll get it for you.'

'Stay put,' said Jacob. 'He'll want to leave immediately.'

'We still have five minutes. I'll be back right away.' She was already on the landing and took the next stairs two steps at a time.

In Olga's room she searched groping among the piles of clothes, swept them from the shelves, dived vainly among the hanging garments. It wasn't until she had pulled up a chair that she found the sweater on a hook in the back of the cupboard. She wanted to take it down quietly and hang it round Olga's shoulders as a surprise.

No longer than a minute did she stand there, catching her breath in the semi-darkness, listening to the cooing of a pigeon on the flat roof, when the silence in the house was broken. Loud voices reached her from the hall, a muffled uproar, and immediately afterwards the slamming of the front door.

'Wait, please wait for me!' she shouted.

She rushed down the stairs but tripped over a loose rod on one of the bottom steps. As she fell, she heard car doors slamming shut. She jumped up and tripped again, this time over a small suitcase which was standing in the middle of the hall. With the sweater clasped against her, she limped to the door.

Looking down the wet, dimly lit quay, all she saw was a grey car slow down and disappear around the corner at the Bastion.

*I*N Uiterwaarden Street, the buildings of the
Social Services and the Municipal Energy Authority stand next to each other, separated by a wide
footpath which runs into the square where the
main entrances are located. Further down on the
same side, the office of Public Housing stands
adjacent to the old low-rise. All three of these
buildings are connected to the municipal heating
system and each has a hot-water vault with
stopcock. In this season the rapidly rising ground
water is heated to boiling-point by pipes which lie
at a depth of two and one half metres and which
have a temperature of 150 ° centigrade. Therefore
the stopcocks can burst and the rising steam
become dangerous for traffic. For this reason the
vaults have to be emptied regularly, a job the
maintenance mechanics had been charged with
that morning.

Behind Public Housing the two men had just placed the red and white gates around the vault and pulled off the cast-iron cover, when a cyclist called out to them: 'Hey there, are the potatoes ready yet?' It turned out to be a friend of Baltus's with whom he had formerly worked in construction. While his partner was extending the hoses to the sewer, Baltus immediately seized the opportunity; he started a lively discussion. The snatches of conversation which Verstrijen caught were enough for him not to join in: again that subcontractor affair. Back at the vault Verstrijen could hardly see the men any more through the widely spreading steam clouds. Heat and cold gripped him at the same time, and for a moment it seemed as if he were overcome by the hot steam as well as by the biting wind. It was a sensation he had never known. He turned towards the building and saw a girl in a big purple sweater who stood looking at him at one of the windows. She shook her head and smiled, and he nodded and thought: I get along everywhere without any trouble, but at home I have nothing but misery. The previous evening it had again been a mess and this morning she hadn't even bothered to get out of bed to fix his bread. It can't go on like that.

'At any rate, you're not bothered by the cold,' shouted Baltus's acquaintance, who had mounted his bicycle again. 'We have our own sauna,' Baltus shouted after him.

Slowly the men set to work. They considered the task they had to carry out as a routine job. Once the immersion pump hangs in the vault, it does the work; the scalding water is automatically carried off to the sewer. As long as you keep your eyes on the whole thing, nothing can go wrong.

When the vault was empty and they had closed it, they shifted their materials towards the Municipal Energy Authority office. Baltus placed the gates against the wall, walked to the car and disappeared into it.

'Hey, aren't you coming back?' called Verstrijen. He received no response and therefore walked to the bus, where Baltus sat staring straight ahead. 'Well, what are you doing?'

'Taking a breather. And thinking things over. Because it's no good.'

'What is no good?' Verstrijen had sat down next to him.

'That system of hot-water vaults. Far too much bother. It can be done very differently.'

'You should have been an inventor.'

'In my opinion, we are the only ones who do it like this. In other places they have solved it in a much more clever way.'

'But that doesn't help us right now.' Verstrijen took the thermos flask and filled the plastic cups.

Baltus had a good gulp. 'The coffee was better early this morning.'

'The service also.'

'How are things at home?'

'Rotten.'

'Again? Well, that blonde at the Salamander could just eat you.'

'Yes, I know that.'

'What's stopping you?' Baltus let the motor run and turned the fan on. The windows fogged.

'I'm beginning to get sick and tired of the cold.' Verstrijen wiped the window with his sleeve.

'It doesn't bother me. I've got a thick hide. But if you ask me: "Do you feel like working today?" Then I say: "No, I don't."'

'Then neither of us feels like it, because I was already fed up when I left the house.'

They chuckled, had another cup of coffee and took out their first sandwich. Verstrijen began to wipe again and peered across the street at the Home for the Aged.

'Nice place. Five floors. I never really noticed it before.'

'Why aren't they connected to the municipal heating?'

'It's a private Home.'

'That's our future, old boy.'

'After you.' Verstrijen opened the car door and looked up. 'The weather is starting to change. We'll get a snowfall. We should get moving.' At any rate he wanted to get back in time to the Salamander.

The deep blue of the frosty sky was already largely covered by racing grey clouds, but sunlight still flashed over the street. And when that happened, the white metal roof edge of the Home glittered.

WITH HER old Persian lamb coat over her arm and her fur hat in her hand, Frieda Borgstein went to the lift, which she entered at the same time as two girls of the household staff who were so deep in conversation that they seemed not to notice her. While the doors were closing, and chattering filled the white steel space, she was assailed by doubts. Why am I doing this? Will I be doing a good thing? Haven't I made a rash decision? she wondered. She closed her eyes and concentrated on the almost motionless descent which she experienced every time as the breathing of a sigh, followed immediately by a feeling of relief on getting out. And when she met the enthusiastically responsive Bien Hijmans in the hall, her hesitation disappeared.

'Well, I thought that it should be done at last. You don't think it's crazy, do you?'

'Crazy?'

'That I suddenly do want it now.'

'It really pleases me.' Bien nodded affectionately at her.

'You must help me, Mrs Hijmans. I'd like to know how many pastries I have to order – also the amount without sugar. And don't forget the staff.'

'I'll see to it. I'll make a list for you.' She was already two steps away.

'Can I get it all quickly? I'm going by Vaissier in a little while.'

'Couldn't you ring them? It's much too cold to go out.'

'Yes, but I also have to make an appointment at the hairdresser.' She edged closer towards Hijmans.

'Can also be done by telephone.' Bien shook her head vigorously. 'Please make it easy for yourself.'

'I have even more to do.' She came closer to Hijmans, as if she didn't want anyone to overhear them, although there was no one to be seen in the hall. 'I have to go to the bank, at any rate.' She said it triumphantly, her head back at an angle.

'It's up to you. But I've warned you.'

'The cold doesn't affect me.'

Bien knew that it made no sense to oppose her. So old and so iron-willed – she had respect for that. 'During coffee I'll come and sit with you and then we can go over everything together. I promise

46

you. Meanwhile you can think about the menu you want for tomorrow. It's your decision.' She placed her red hand on Frieda's shoulder and before walking away she stooped quickly. 'You've dropped your fur hat.'

'Oh, am I scattering things again? Just give it to me. I'll put it away.' She crumpled the hat into her coat pocket and watched the disappearing Hijmans, flapping apron-coat and all. She was always in a hurry. After each word you exchanged with her she took a step away from you, as if she were forever on her way, pushed along by her task of taking everything and everyone under her wings.

always in hurry

always in a hurry

Just as Frieda was about to enter the lounge, she spotted Ben Abels. He was busy at a meter cupboard, his tool-box on the floor next to him. She had known him since 1938, when he had come as youngest employee into Jacob's office – a thin, shy, seventeen-year-old who had not known what to do with his adoration for Olga.

'You are going out this early, Mrs Borgstein?'

'Yes, I'll risk it after the coffee, although everyone says that the weather is too severe for me.'

'And you make light of that?'

'Oh Ben, I have so much planned. I have to go to the bank, to the hairdresser, to Vaissier, to. . . .' There was still something else that she wanted to do, she couldn't remember what.

'Don't bite off more than you can chew!' He smiled. In the vertical wrinkles of his face the white stubble of his beard stood in sharp contrast to the leathery skin. He always reminded her of a sailor, but that was because she knew that he had gone to sea. Nothing in his demeanour recalled the awkward, ever absent-minded lad he had been; only the bashfulness she could still sometimes detect. That was dear to her. It belonged to the past.

When after thirty years Abels returned to his native town, he had obtained a job as Jack of all trades in the Home whose new wing still had to be built. After his liberation from the camp, he and other typhus patients had been nursed in a hospital in the south. Two pieces of news reached him which caused him to leave the country: he alone of his family had survived the war, and the belongings from his parents' house had vanished. He signed on with a freighter, and after a number of trips he remained in the United States. There he had gone through a hundred jobs, been married and divorced, been poverty-stricken and fairly well off, and had ended up driving a truck with which he criss-crossed the northern states for so long that he could no longer bear to see a highway. Urged by a friend, he went with him to Brazil, thought that he had finally found peace in an organization run by Dutch farmers. But when, during a yearly market in the neighbouring town, he recognized one of his camp guards – 'Der Knüppel', 'the Club' – among the rancheros, he decided that the time had come to take an aeroplane back.

It took him by surprise to encounter Olga's mother at the Home. That she was still alive.

'You knew Hein Kessels, didn't you?' she had asked after they had exchanged their stories for the first time.

'From the office. He worked for his father. He was also in the housing division.'

'What did you think of him?'

'Something of a braggart. He wore those light suits . . .'

'I mean, could you imagine that he would go and work for the Germans?'

'No – honestly, not for one moment.'

'My husband trusted him completely. For six thousand guilders he was going to take us to Switzerland.'

'That's the way it went. Crazier amounts have been asked. There were those who set others up, who brought you false papers and then tipped off the Nazis that you wanted to leave the country illegally.'

'It happened so fast. Before I was downstairs they were gone.' She stared at the back of her left hand, rubbed the loose skin with her fingertips as if she were counting the bones. 'They always took everyone away, didn't they? Why not me? I have never understood it.'

Who has ever understood it? thought Abels.

She had expected that they would come back to collect her. Until darkness fell she had remained standing in the doorway, looking out over the glistening quay, the black water of the river, at the row of houses on the other side which took on the aspect of a brick wall. The rain lashed her face. Nowhere was there a strip of light, nowhere a person. Jacob must have said that I was still at home? First, she left the door open a crack; later, it was already past twelve, she closed it. Jacob must have said that I was not there! But she would not let them go alone. Early the next morning she would immediately report herself. The pain in her swollen ankle increased. She could no longer stand on her foot.

The next morning she was found by the book-keeper, who still came by every day to keep Jacob up to date on the state of affairs at the office. She no longer knew how they had moved her from there and how she had finally landed at the Oosterveens'.

'You know, Ben,' she said musing, 'what amazes me most is our memory, how it works. Why you forget one thing and remember another.'

He nodded. She need not tell him any more.

When shortly after that she found him with his sleeves rolled up busy unplugging her sink, she spotted the number on his arm.

'Let me see,' she said. It slipped out before she

suddenly looks away

knew. Timidly he turned his arm towards her. She cast a cursory glance at it and immediately looked away, whereupon he quickly rolled down his sleeve. There were those who had let it be removed, but sailors are used to tattoos, she realized. Not until a few years later – they were already in the new building – had she asked him that absurd question: whether he had perhaps encountered one of the others over there. He had merely shaken his head. After that they had never again spoken about that period.

ask more questions –

She walked back to the meter cupboard with him and suddenly placed her hand on his arm. 'You're coming tomorrow, I hope?'

'What do you mean? Where?'

'To coffee.'

'Is there something to celebrate, by any chance?'

'Tomorrow I'll be eighty-five, Ben. I want to do something about it this time.'

'Eighty-five? I thought you were in your late seventies.'

'Come on.' Slightly giggly, she nudged him. 'I'm not saying anything about it yet in there.' She pointed in the direction of the lounge. 'Won't they be surprised when the platters with pastries are carried in? Just watch them.' And, bending towards him, she asked: 'Keep it to yourself for now, won't you?'

'Not a word. You can count on me.' While she shuffled away, her slender back very briefly reminded him of young Frieda Borgstein's silhouette. 'Your coat!' he called out. 'It's dragging on the floor.'

'So what, that old thing,' she said. Her hand made a gesture of discard. 'I don't have to wear it to a reception any more.' She continued dragging the coat along.

From the shaking of her shoulders he could tell that she was laughing to herself.

*A*FTER THE mechanics had again disappeared into the car Mr Marks, who had observed the activities from his room on the first floor, went downstairs to drink coffee.

'In this temperature, that doesn't look like an unpleasant job to me. Did you see them at it?' He took his usual seat opposite Frieda Borgstein and gestured with his thumb to the window wall.

'I have a view of it from upstairs.' She said it blandly and turned back towards the lounge entrance to see if Hijmans had yet arrived.

'Do you mean the vaults where they are working?' A man with a pale, bony face and a pointed nose shuffled on wool slippers up to Mr Marks, who had opened his newspaper. 'A fine system to heat these large buildings. They've really invented something.' He remained standing behind Mr Marks and glanced at the paper.

'I'm always glad when something is happening in the street,' said a woman with a Groningen accent. 'Aren't they late with the coffee this morning?'

'"Electric rates remain high for industrial customers,"' read the man behind Marks, articulating stiffly. 'At least we don't have that worry.' He bent further forward, held on to his glasses. '"And, Joep, were you cold last night?"' He started laughing, with hiccups.

Abruptly Mr Marks put down his newspaper. 'That is a vulgar advertisement.' He looked at his table companion and spotted the coat on the chair next to her. 'Plans today?'

The man who had been reading aloud, remained bent forward, momentarily bewildered, then shuffled back to his seat, grumbling.

'Yes, I have a lot to do. I'm leaving after the coffee.'

'You don't mean that.' He leant solicitously towards her. 'Why should you go out in that nasty wind?'

'Please let me decide.' Her tone remained friendly. She kept her eyes on the door.

'She has to go to the hairdresser, Louis,' called out the lady from Groningen, Marks's cousin, who often showed jealousy because he paid more attention to Borgstein than to her.

'Selma, please!' He wanted to prevent disturbing Frieda's clearly pleasant mood. Lately she had an even greater tendency to be aloof. When they had both just come to the Home, they had called each other by their first names, went walking together regularly, now and then had tea somewhere. He found her to be an intelligent woman with whom, despite her reserve, he had a pleasant relationship. Once he had casually asked her if she would care to marry him. He realized, he said, that it must take her by surprise, but basically their backgrounds differed very little, and hadn't they had the same experiences? They would be able to lay claim to one of the handsome two-person apartments, and he was willing to admit honestly to her that being alone oppressed him. Didn't they get along well with each other?

Frieda wouldn't hear of it, and she rejected his offer in a few words: her room suited her fine and she was set on her privacy. Afterwards they gradually went walking together less often.

He had retained only his seat next to her at dinner and opposite her at coffee. In retrospect he wasn't too sorry that nothing had come of it, for she began to behave with increasing obstinacy and showed that she had no real interest in him and just as little in the other residents. The only one with whom she was on familiar terms was the handyman Abels.

'They couldn't get me out of the door with a stick. You can catch something just like that,' he

55

said. He smoothed the newspaper, wiped the palm of his hand clean and, as though he had forced it, began coughing violently.

'I can understand that. It wouldn't do for you. But I can't afford to stay indoors today.'

'Stay indoors? Do we have to stay indoors?' It was the cracking voice of a small, thin woman with hair trimmed straight, whose bright-green dress was almost painfully out of harmony with the subdued colours that dominated the lounge. 'We have stayed indoors long enough.'

'That time is past,' someone consoled her.

'Nothing is past, nothing is past!' She had jumped up and looked around, waving her arms wildly. Even though they were used to such scenes from her, there was still a certain embarrassment in their reaction to it. One or two tried to calm her, but most took no notice of the incident. Certainly not Frieda Borgstein. She was first to see the director's light-blue suit appear next to the coffee-cart in the hall.

It was four minutes past ten. While the girls balanced the white trays above the white heads, Rena van Straten walked to the middle of the room and announced that the foreign visitors would come half an hour earlier. Therefore they could eat at twelve-thirty as usual.

'They must be in a hurry,' said the woman from Groningen, and, to her cousin: 'Louis, now we can play bridge at our usual time after all.'

56

'Where are they from?' asked a woman with huge glasses.

'From Sweden, Mrs Krijger.' Van Straten moved smilingly among the tables, moving a vase here, straightening an empty chair there, and for everyone who asked she had brief, precise information, conveyed in such a light-hearted tone that it seemed as if she were constantly telling jokes.

'Are they doing a house-search?' shouted the woman in the green dress. 'They won't find anything in my place. I've disposed of everything.'

'You needn't worry about anything. Nothing will happen here.' The director took the woman's hand and gave it a soothing pat. 'Just drink your coffee quietly.'

'The liquid that works miracles.' Marks winked at Frieda, but she didn't see it, only the door existed for her. What was the matter with her and what was she waiting for?

Rena van Straten knew that the agitation which she detected all around her would disappear after the second cup of coffee. 'We'll carry on as usual,' she said emphatically. 'Aren't we used to this kind of visit by now?' Walking to the door, she saw Frieda's coat lying on the chair. 'Are you going out, Mrs Borgstein?'

'I'm still waiting a moment for Mrs Hijmans and then I'm going out, yes.'

'Then you are the only one today, I think.'

'That could easily be.'

'Is there no one who wants to go with you?' And when she noticed that no one took the hint: 'Can I perhaps send one of the girls along?'

'I always go alone, you know that. I like it.' She held both hands round her coffee-cup and drank with small sips, compassionately looking up at the newspaper behind which Marks had hidden himself very obviously.

'Mrs Borgstein wants nothing to do with these gentlemen – right, Mrs Borgstein? When they come you'll be gone, and by the time you come home they will be gone. That's how it is,' said Mrs Krijger tartly.

'Do wrap up warmly at any rate,' advised the director, 'with an extra sweater over your dress.'

'Will they be looking at our rooms?' someone asked.

'I have already explained all that to you.' Van Straten's voice sounded excessively patient as she pointed out once more that no one would be inconvenienced. 'If the gentlemen just want to peek in here and there, you certainly wouldn't have any objection to it.'

Frieda Borgstein put down her cup, picked up her handbag and stood up. 'I have forgotten something,' she said to Mr Marks.

*L*UCKILY it had dawned on her in time: she had left everything out. That never happened to her. She never left her room without putting away her belongings. The table was covered with the family photographs which she regularly laid out as though it were a game of solitaire. The notebook with her calculations was lying open. The thought of strangers prying into it made her heart beat too fast. She put the photographs back into the leather case and stored the notebook in the drawer of the cabinet. The drawer stuck when she pushed it shut, causing the portraits on top to shift. She straightened them and took Jacob's portrait in her hands.

She would not dare tell anyone what she had been doing with it the last two years, afraid that they would consider her mad. But there were so many things she could no longer do at her age that one day she had simply given in to impulse: she slipped the portrait, frame and all into her handbag, in which it fitted exactly, and took it along when she went for a walk. It became a habit. Weather permitting, she walked to the river. Opposite their old house she would sit down on a bench by the quay and look at the barges going up and down the river in a solemn rhythm, journeys which had always been there and would always go on. This way she had the feeling that Jacob also continued to share in what they had seen for so long from those upstairs windows.

Without hesitating she put the portrait and the leather case with the photographs into her handbag. She flipped open the silver cigarette-case with the initials J.B., sniffed it, stretched the elastic fasteners and stuck it in the compartment next to the portrait. During breakfast she had made up her mind to walk to the river again and to walk down the quay after her errands. That was what she had wanted to tell Ben Abels! They held hands and watched Leo who constantly ran ahead, using the mooring-posts to play leap-frog, and had to be pulled back whenever he walked with outstretched arms on the narrow granite edge of the quay. The evening that she herself had stood there the street lights had been off. She had considered this as a sign. But she had not been able to bring herself to take that step.

Looking for a sweater in the cupboard, she felt

60

herself becoming resentful because the director had needed to advise her to put on more clothes. Why hadn't she thought of it herself? She was allergic to good advice. While she was putting on her sweater, she saw how above the buildings the clouds were blowing apart like curtains. A streak of sunlight quickly edged over the empty table.

Downstairs she heard from Mr Marks that Bien Hijmans had come to ask for her.

'What a pity. Couldn't she have waited for me for a moment?'

'Hijmans and waiting? That doesn't rhyme. But she would be back right away, she said.'

'I hope so.'

'It's good that you've put on a sweater. I had wanted to mention it to you, but Van Straten anticipated me of course.'

She let that go. One of the girls brought her another cup of coffee which she picked up with trembling hands. Nothing ever escaped him, he was always looking after her, he always wanted to assist her. 'Can I be of any help?' was his stock question. She was glad she would be able to go out before long, out from this room in which everyone meddled with everyone else. Around her they were talking about Sweden, and the fact that they knew so little about it. They knew so much more about another holiday destination: Israel.

That was predictable, they tried to surpass each other. And then followed the European countries, with the capitals, the sights, the connections. She felt as if she were in a geography class. 'Switzerland' she caught.

'And you, Mrs Borgstein?'

She shook her head. She could have gone to Australia, but that would have been a flight for which she would never have forgiven herself. Uncertainty about her decision again crept into her mind. What did she think she was doing? For whom was she doing it all? Her gaze strayed to the newspaper behind which Marks had withdrawn for the umpteenth time, to the headline above an article: *Builder fraud made fools of us all.* Seven words, twenty-eight letters; if she subtracted one from the other it would come to twenty-one. It all worked out. It had been the evening of the twenty-first. Their wedding anniversary would fall three days later. They were to celebrate it on the way. 'And when we are in Switzerland, we'll do it once more,' Jacob had said.

Why had she remained standing in Olga's room? Why hadn't she walked downstairs immediately? She could have gained at least a minute. She shivered and did up the top buttons of her sweater. Until the end of her days two images would continue to appear and sometimes shift over each other, just as now: she stood on the threshold of a crowded room and could not go in; she stood on

the threshold of her empty house and could not go
out. Through the rear window of the car as it
drove away she saw their heads moving. But she
was deluding herself; she hadn't really been able
to see them, for the distance had been too great.

*T*HE LOUNGE emptied gradually and most of the residents went back to their rooms. Mr Marks was still sitting opposite Frieda whose absent-mindedness gave him the uneasy feeling that they didn't share the same space. She stared ahead and from time to time rubbed the table-cloth. That rubbing especially made him nervous. He began to fold his newspaper, but suddenly threw the paper down, pushed his chair back with a jerk and hurried to the door. Already half-way in the hall he called back, attentive to the last: 'I think that Hijmans is coming.' She started up and saw his bald, freckled scalp turned towards her as if he were bowing.

She had already put on her coat, which she was now impatiently buttoning and unbuttoning. She took her scarf off and looked at her watch. It was becoming increasingly late and she just sat here. Maybe Hijmans had forgotten her.

It must have been shortly before that twenty-first of April that she had sat waiting for Jacob and the children. They had gone into town and had stayed away much longer than had been agreed. A growing feeling of oppression kept her motionless in her chair at the kitchen table. She concentrated on the tap with the worn-out washer, and began counting the drops of water which fell slowly into the sink. She had counted long past a hundred when she heard the front door opening.

'We made a detour,' explained Jacob. 'We had to. There was trouble again. They are picketing in front of stores.'

'Before long we shan't be able to go out on the street at all any more.' Leo looked dejected and Olga was angry. 'We met our former neighbours. They looked the other way when they saw us. It's just as well we're leaving soon.'

'Hey, are you still there?' said a voice next to her. It was Mrs Krijger, who had left something. 'You should really hurry. Before long you'll run into them, and you don't want that, do you?' Flourishing a magazine, she wobbled off.

That Krijger woman certainly doesn't understand things at all, thought Frieda. Why should I hurry? I can go this afternoon just as well. They are quite welcome to come to my rooms. I have cleared everything away. She began to feel warm in her heavy sweater. She unbuttoned it and stood up. She would not wait any longer.

The glass doors swung open and Bien Hijmans, her face flushed red, came towards Frieda at such a speed that the latter retreated slightly. Mrs Borgstein must not think that she had been forgotten, absolutely not, but everyone in this place needed her at the same time, and what did she think of asparagus soup to start with and then veal stew with small green peas and salad and a special dessert and the table decorated, of course, and surely she wanted to sit at the head? Together they had walked up to the couch next to the entrance. Frieda put her handbag down. She had been able only to nod in response to the eruption of Hijmans.

'Should you really do all this, Mrs Borgstein? It's going to cost you a fortune. Look right here.' Bien gave her a note.

'I would have to put my glasses on for that.' Frieda slipped the piece of paper into her coat pocket. 'After all, didn't I want this myself? No one is forcing me.'

'Good, such a special birthday, it should be celebrated. You are, I believe, the third oldest here. But pastry is so expensive nowadays. I understand quite well. You want to choose it yourself at Vaissier. Such a confectioner is hard to find nowadays.' She helped Frieda with her coat, did up the top buttons, arranged her scarf. 'Well, now you're warm. Do go soon. Fortunately it's in ·the neighbourhood.' She coaxed the old woman, who had accepted this attention, half resigned, half annoyed, to the hall. The manner in which Bien, as a finishing touch, pulled up the collar of her coat – as though she had been dressing a doll – provoked a defensive gesture from Frieda which escaped Hijmans. Her apron-coat was flapping once again.

Coming out of her office, the director saw Frieda standing in the hall. She was busy putting on her gloves. From that distance it looked as though her diminutive figure in the long coat, under the hat which had become too wide, remained upright solely because of that black wrapping.

'Are you going?' The director walked towards her.

'Yes, I'm going.' It sounded firm. She had had her doubts, she admitted that, but wasn't she used to taking a morning walk? And everyone acted as if she were going to undertake something extraordinary. These Swedes would not miss her, and at any rate they now had one less nuisance. She tried to adopt her usual tone, but her turned-up collar smothered her voice.

Rena let her hand move over the worn sleeve of the Persian lamb coat. 'Well, go ahead then. And take good care of yourself.'

'I always do.'

They nodded at each other. They smiled. Frieda walked to the exit. 'I'll be back on time,' she added.

The director heard no more. In her office the sharp buzzer of the intercom had rung. Could she please come to the second floor? they asked. Time was pressing.

'JUST THE Social Services to empty and then we're off,' said Baltus. After working on the second vault, they had again gone to sit in the bus.

'If that were possible.' Verstrijen had his doubts about it.

'Do you know what's wrong?' Baltus took his own thermos flask and poured some coffee out once again. 'Those subcontractors couldn't beat it.' He hit his knee with his fist. 'Oh man, the whole bunch is as corrupt as the plague.'

Verstrijen didn't react. Although he was irritated at not being able to see out, he no longer took the trouble to wipe the fogged windscreen. He was fed up. You couldn't get anywhere with this job. Something which had never happened to them before: the immersion pump had failed several times, and a hose had torn loose. They had had to sprinkle sand, for the water streaming over the pavement froze as you watched. Once the morning was over, they could perhaps finally unhook.

The equipment was already laid out at the vault of the Social Services. Baltus checked the immersion pump, to be on the safe side. 'I want no more aggravation with that thing. What if we had to go back to get another one?'

'Where did you leave the gates?' asked Verstrijen.

'They're already in the back of the bus.'

'Won't we need them here?'

'Certainly not. Not next to this vault. Who would creep alongside it? With the car in front, there's almost no room, a child can see that.' With a hook Baltus lifted up the lid and pushed it next to the vault, from which white clouds of steam whirled up. He walked towards the footpath between the buildings.

'Where are you going?'

'To the Energy Office men's room.'

'Again?'

'Young man, you've got to understand, I'm as strong as a horse, but I have a weak bladder. That's my trouble.'

'And that open vault?'

'Aren't you standing next to it? Is there something wrong with your eyes?'

'You should have left the lid on for the time being.'

'Nonsense. It can blow off steam till I get back.'

Verstrijen watched his partner walk away with small, stiff steps and disappear into the building through a side door. The hot steam from the vault came straight towards him. For a few seconds he was completely enveloped in it. Blindly he stepped back, rubbed his face and dabbed his weeping eyes with his knuckles. Stupid of him to stand facing the wind. Again he had that disquieting experience of heat and cold overcoming him at the same time and turning him into jelly.

He began pacing up and down, his jacket collar up, his hands in his pockets. He was shivery, he wanted a cigarette, but he thought it too cold to roll one. He stopped on the lid of the Energy Office vault and scanned the front of the building. Maybe some good-looking girl with a cute sweater would appear again at a window. If she smiled at him, that would be fine. But all he saw was a stern-looking man in a dark suit who glanced at him and turned away at once. The creep.

I shouldn't have done it, he thought. You solved nothing that way. With his coat already on, he had walked to the bedroom. He knew she was pretending to sleep and it had driven him wild all over again. He had dragged her out of bed and for a moment had not known what to do with the warm, sleepy body. Then he had cut loose. As she fell back on the covers he stormed out of the door.

The church clock showed a quarter to eleven. 16:45 Yet it seemed as if they already had a whole workday behind them. He felt his face becoming numb in the biting wind, but at least there was warmth under his feet and from where he stood he could easily watch the vault.

ON LEAVING the Home, Frieda Borgstein was caught in a gust of wind which seemed to plunge down on her from the roof of the building. It took her breath away, but she didn't think of choosing the shelter of the overhang at the entrance. She gripped the collar of her coat, pressed her handbag, whose handle she had pushed up to her shoulder, tightly against her and prepared to cross the street.

The sight of the grey car on the other side of the street made her hesitate on the kerb. Was it still there? Was it the same one she had seen appearing out of the dark that morning? They had parked it in front of the footpath in such a way that she was confused for a moment. Maybe the path was closed off and she would have to take the long way round. That didn't suit her at all now that she had been delayed for almost half an hour.

She hid her face even deeper inside her coat collar so that only her eyes remained free, and crossed the street.

In the middle of the road a sudden gust gripped her with such force that she had difficulty in staying on her feet. It pushed her to the other side, so that she once again became uncertain on approaching the car. Should she pass along the front of the vehicle or behind it? The wind left her no choice, drove her to the left, to the back of the bus.

The courier of the messenger service drove into Uiterwaarden Street on his heavy moped. Under the black, one-piece helmet his head hung close above the handlebars. Behind him swished his walkie-talkie aerial. A pennant hung from it, bearing the name of his volley-ball club. He was slowing down to turn into the first side-street on the left, where he had to stop at a number of offices, when he saw ahead of him a woman dressed in black crossing the street. You couldn't really call it crossing the street, she was being blown across the road as though she were weightless.

At the same time he spotted the Volkswagen bus and remembered that one of the mechanics had said that he could come and warm his hands with them. A joke, he had thought. Now it appeared that the source of heat was located between the car and the Social Services building, where a column of steam was blowing in shreds against the façade. Giving full throttle, he raced into the side-street. In a little while he would definitely like to see what those two were up to.

Bien Hijmans had fled from the kitchen. During the writing up of the menus for the next day, she had been exasperated by the noise that reigned there. The radio droned, dishes clattered, and above it all rang out the shrill voices of the staff who were involved in a heated discussion. At first she thought they were fighting, but when she realized that their excitement was about the latest instalment of an American TV series, she lost her temper. Screaming and stamping she told them to shut up and turned off the radio. One of the girls still tried to tell her that the big dishwasher was out of order, but she pushed her aside, shouting that she didn't want to hear another word, and escaped. She had to go to her room, she had to be alone for a moment.

By the lift she met the director, who let her enter first with a gesture that could be called light-hearted. From the way that Rena looked at her flushed face, Bien saw that Rena knew: Hijmans had again made a scene. But her tact – the quality which Bien disliked most – prevented her from making any comment. She pushed the 2 button and looked at her watch. 'Twelve minutes to eleven. Let's hope they're on time.'

'They'd better be.' Bien took a few deep breaths. She felt her temper fading, passed her hand over her sweating forehead, puffed.

Again Rena pretended not to notice anything. 'Will I see you straight away on the first floor?' The lift stopped. She stepped into the hall and said: 'Borgstein did go out after all.'

'I know. It will be harder than she expected, I'm afraid.'

'I'd intended to watch her from my window. Actually I always do watch when they cross the street. But I was needed here.'

'I'll be with you in a minute. I'm going to freshen up a bit. My hair!' She pulled at her curls. Before the doors closed she had a good look at Rena's beaming face. Under the cheek-bones her cheeks showed a light blush which was not exclusively due to her make-up. She's looking forward to another meeting with her boy-friend, De Vlonder, thought Bien. She pushed the knob for the fifth floor. The fragrance of a discreet perfume hung in the lift.

Ben Abels sat bent over the motor of the dishwasher. Shortly before, while walking through the hall, he had seen the glass door close behind Frieda Borgstein. His impulse to follow her had been strong. Couldn't he perfectly well take her in the car? It was no weather for such a person. But he had to go to the kitchen for a rush job. Nothing must go wrong today.

Maybe she wouldn't even have wanted it. Take me? I don't like to be held by the hand. He had come to know her as self-willed, sometimes slightly authoritarian, but also warm-hearted, considerate, ready to help him get over his idiotic shyness. In doing so she sometimes took drastic measures. He still remembered how she – short and delicate, but dominantly present in the rooms filled with guests in the house on Zuid Quay – had extricated herself from a small group when she saw him, awkward with his bunch of flowers, standing at the door. 'Come on in, Ben. We're not celebrating in the hall.' She was wearing a cream-coloured blouse and her dark hair was combed back tightly in a knot. What was it that reminded him of the odours in that room? A bewildering aroma of wine, cigar-smoke, pineapples and nuts came towards him in a wave of warmth as she took him by the hand and gave him a seat at the table, directly opposite Olga, who scrutinized him with a look so amused and at the same time so penetrating that he became red to the roots of his hair. Mechanically busy with the motor which began to hum again, he wondered to whom he had been more attracted at that time – to Frieda or to her daughter. He resolved to bring flowers for her tomorrow.

Throughout the first morning hours Carla hadn't had enough hands. The location of the Salamander, near the river and the industrial areas, and the nature of the establishment, a cross between an old-fashioned café and a snack-bar, provided for a large clientele. She had broken three coffee-cups, spilled hot water on her fingers and had made several mistakes in settling bills. It was not because of the rush; she was used to that.

Her thoughts had been on the two men who, with their early arrival, had started the day and upset her. Baltus, an indifferent bear of a man, mainly interested in his food and drink, left her cold. It was Verstrijen who mattered. She had never known him to be as dour as she had seen him this morning. She knew that he was regularly at loggerheads with his wife, but he seldom gave any hint of it. On the other hand, his intentions towards her were quite clear; and she admitted that she was susceptible to them. She had fallen for him.

When things calmed down a bit around ten and the boss appeared, she said that she urgently needed to go to the Public Housing Office regarding the application for her new apartment. He granted her request anything but whole-heartedly. Before he could change his mind, she swopped her shoes for brown fleece boots and put on her imitation leopardskin coat.

The cold did her good. With tingling cheeks, her blonde hair blowing from under her leopardskin cap, she walked briskly to the bus-stop. When she gave the driver her strip of tickets, he immediately grabbed her hand and asked if she would be free that evening.

'Yes,' she said, 'but not for you.' Laughing to herself she looked for a seat. The day promised to turn out differently from what she had thought possible in the morning.

Verstrijen was standing in the cold on the vault lid. Baltus was making him wait. Of course he had again found someone on whom he could vent his spleen about the subcontractor affair. As if there was nothing else to worry about. It was getting a bit much. Before you knew it he would get pneumonia, just because that fathead was slacking off. He was going to bring him back.

As he turned towards the footpath, jerking his shoulders angrily, he thought he noticed a dark spot out of the corner of his left eye, something that was blowing across the street. But the bus blocked his view and he paid no further attention to it.

*T*HE WIND was everywhere. It circled around her, it pursued her until she stood between the wall of the office building and the Volkswagen. Not until then did it leave her alone. Surprised, she experienced the sudden calm in which she could hear the wheezing of her breath. She wanted to get out her handkerchief but decided not to; it was better to hold her handbag shut. With the back of her hand in its woollen glove she wiped her eyes, which had become wet, giving her the impression that everything ahead of her was blanketed in a mist. At that moment she spotted the steaming vault. While crossing the street she had not formed a clear idea of the source of the clouds of steam which she had seen rising above the bus. Although the realization took her off guard, it did not discourage her. Now that she was here, she had to go on. She thought that she could easily pass it. She had at least the space of half a metre.

Maybe she misjudged the space. Maybe it was because of her eyes, which she had been unable to dry. It is possible that she tripped over the hose which lay next to the vault, or over the lid. A combination of causes is not out of the question. The true facts of the case will never be established. At any rate she had not taken more than two or three steps before she felt the ground give way under her feet.

Verstrijen was not yet half-way down the footpath when he heard a weak cry behind him. He turned round. He was at once aware that the sound could have come from nowhere but the open vault and that it had to do with the black something which had appeared earlier in the left corner of his field of vision. Running to the vault he realized that they should have put the gates up. Baltus had placed them in the back of the bus. And he would never forgive Baltus for not being here now.

While he was searching in the steam for the climbing irons installed against the concrete wall, he knew it would be impossible to get someone out of the vault without help. Shouting and cursing he descended to the churning ground water in which, hanging forward as far as he could, he began to grope. It was hell down there. He had to squeeze his eyes shut against the scalding steam, which cut off his breath. He reached around blindly, felt something, an article of clothing, and pulled it. It slipped from his hands as he lost his work glove. With a second attempt he seemed to succeed. He got hold of an arm, dragged it above water and straightened himself. 'Come here, grab it!' he screamed when he realized that he wouldn't be able to climb up with his load. He couldn't hold it, he couldn't reach the next iron, had to let go and heard again the splash of the body.

Crying with frustration and anger, he stuck his head above the edge of the vault, bent it deep towards the pavement to avoid the steam, which was choking him. He understood that for the person who lay down there it would be too late if help didn't come immediately. Now that the wind gripped him again, he felt for the third time how heat and cold together overcame him. Not until afterwards did he feel the smarting pain on his face, arms and legs. Through the clouds of steam he saw the shoes of the bystanders, who formed an immobile circle one metre away. What he didn't understand was where they had come from so fast, and even less why they didn't lift a finger to help, letting him lie forward on the bricks. Shitting cowards.

'The fire department,' he shouted. 'The fire department!'

Someone had already called them, they said.

*I*T CANNOT be established exactly which one of
the residents first discovered that something had
happened in the street. Later, disagreement seems
to have arisen about who realized immediately that
it was connected with Frieda Borgstein. After coffee
they had as usual gone to their rooms to put things
in order before taking their regular places at the
window. They spent the rest of the morning there.
Usually little that happened in the street escaped
their notice. But this time no one had seen Frieda
cross the street.

Not even Mr Marks. Around that time he was
in the bathroom. He had suffered a renewed attack
of intestinal cramp, more severe than in the lounge,
which he had had to leave in a hurry. Dejected by
this discomfort which threatened to become chronic,
he had locked the door, taken pills again and had
waited for the pain to ease.

He had lost interest in the work at the vaults. These men slacked off in a disgraceful way. Quickly set down a pump and then into the bus; quickly shift a hose and again into the bus. It had begun to irritate him. He went back to his armchair with _Christian Wahnschaffe_, a book he had read again and again since his young days, and looked outside in passing, hoping to catch the mechanics at their umpteenth coffee-break. That is why it gave him a slight start to see a throng of people standing on the other side of the street. From their behaviour he gathered that something had happened. Perhaps a worker's accident. It must have happened behind the Volkswagen bus, beside the vault from which he saw the steam floating above the heads of the onlookers.

Scanning the street in both directions – where were the police? – his eye was caught by a young woman who came walking hurriedly. She wore some sort of tiger coat. He bent forward so as to follow her better. A pleasant, rather showy-looking figure, he thought. At the Energy Office she started running. Her fair hair blew from under her hat, which she held with one hand.

Mr Marks put down his book. He sat down and got up again.

The stops at offices took longer than the courier of the messenger service had imagined. At several firms he was asked to wait for documents which had to be delivered elsewhere. When he could finally start up his moped, he heard a siren and saw a fire-engine with its blue flashing light cross the intersection. At full speed he drove out of the street, took too wide a turn and was almost grazed by a black Mercedes coming from the right. The driver angrily shook his fist at him.

Jesus, he had come within a hair-breadth of being a client of the Health Service. No brakes! In reaction he continued riding provokingly close to the car. The two in the back seat wore fur hats; the hothead behind the wheel, a checked cap. His thin, grey hair stuck out over his collar.

Through the windscreen the boy saw that the fire-engine had stopped where the mechanics were working. He shot out from behind the car.

*W*HEN THE director noticed that the lift was at the fifth floor, she decided not to wait but to take the stairs to the first. They were not on time. Calling too late to say that you're coming half an hour earlier and then still not keeping the appointment, that she thought was most irregular. No matter how much she liked De Vlonder, she would make that clear to him, he could count on it.

During her inspection of the two-person apartments she had let herself be delayed by a married couple who greeted her with a two-voiced 'God morgon. Hur mår Ni?' – especially rehearsed for the Swedish visitors. She was so touched by it that she had not been able to break away immediately.

The shrill voice of Gerrie reached her as she was half-way down the stairs. Rena could not understand what she was shouting. It was unusual for her to shout. There was to be no shouting in the halls, where the rooms of the residents were situated. The members of the staff had been carefully instructed on that point. It alarmed her, all the more so since a moment earlier she had caught the wail of a siren.

All at once a multitude of sounds came at her, travelling from floor to floor. Everywhere doors opened, bumping noises came from the rooms, coming and going. Somewhere a heavy object toppled. People pushed bells and called out to each other; screams echoed through the smooth cylinder of the stairwell, while in contrast sounded the calming voices of the attendants, as if they were beginning a canon.

Meanwhile Bien Hijmans was in the lift. She was well groomed for her, had rubbed cream into her rough hands, taken off her eternal apron-coat and, inspired by Rena, had made unsparing use of cologne. Suspecting nothing, she arrived at the first floor when she heard the alarmed shouting of the girl and the wave of turmoil which travelled through the building.

Gerrie had gone into the reception-room with a tray full of coffee things and, curious to see whether the visitors were arriving, had walked to the window. The chaotic spectacle awaiting her in the normally quiet street had upset her. Later she said that it was like going into a cinema when the film has already started and the images sweep over you unexpectedly: blue, flashing lights, ladders, ropes, a swelling crowd moving aside for three firemen equipped with breathing apparatus, the steaming vault which, after the Volkswagen bus had backed up, had been hidden again by the fire-engine. She thought that was the scariest: she could only guess what was happening behind it.

Van Straten and Hijmans stood at the window of the reception-room. They looked at each other. They both knew who was involved, but it was as though they wanted to exorcize their knowledge. The name did not pass their lips.

'I've had a premonition all morning.' Bien gripped Rena's arm, who disengaged herself brusquely.

'Where is Abels?' Rena asked the girl.

'In the kitchen,' said Gerrie. She had remained on the threshold.

'Go and warn him. Let him go and have a look.'

'He is already outside,' said Hijmans, 'and the visitors are arriving.'

Abels had had misgivings. On hearing the siren he had become worried, and when the sound stopped right in front of the Home he didn't think twice; he went to the hall.

Through the glass doors he saw four men against

the background of a red truck. Three of them were about to enter. He slipped past them. The fourth – short, stocky, with thin grey hair hanging down his neck – remained standing on the pavement, looking across the street. Because he turned round abruptly, Abels looked him in the eye. The man's face was vaguely familiar to him.

*O*N THE DAY of the funeral it was still eight degrees or so below freezing, but the wind had subsided, the sky was uniformly blue. Abels had taken the bus to the cemetery and stood <u>alone</u> in front of the entrance gate, looking from the raised roadway over a line of young birch trees, widely separated trunks whose separateness was emphasized by the thin sunlight. When a girl and a boy, who had stepped off the bus with him, ran into the wood, dodging among the trees, it seemed for a moment as though the trees moved closer together.

A car parked carefully on the sloping bank. He heard the crunching of the layer of ice under the wheels. The driver, a man of around fifty in a dark coat and an old-fashioned hat, was accompanied by a young man and a young woman. They came to the gate, stood next to him and nodded at him as if they knew him. He nodded back.

His fear was confirmed by a motor cyclist dressed in black leather who had obviously seen him come out of the home. 'An old woman fell into the vault,' he shouted. 'They've just pulled her out.' After he had pushed through the crowd to the spot where she lay, a municipal works mechanic asked if he knew the victim. The firemen had wrapped her in a heavy cloth which left free only her now almost unrecognizable face. What would stick in his mind for ever was the look of bewilderment around the mouth, from which trickled some rust-coloured water, and the shabby hair, plastered against the scalp. At that moment she was still alive. It had begun to snow. Thin flakes fell on her. Her eyelids seemed to tremble. As they carried her to the ambulance, he saw her handbag lying on the ground. He picked it up. It was heavy with moisture, the leather had burst.

The mechanic who had spoken to him used a hook to push the lid over the vault. He looked like a strong man but his motions were helpless, shaky, and he spoke haltingly. 'There goes my partner,' he said. 'He's got second-degree burns, they say. And no one lifted a finger to help him. They let you go to hell, dammit.' He stamped on the lid. The partner, his face swollen and contorted by pain, was being led away by a male nurse from the Health Department. He held his hands up stiffly, as though he couldn't move them any more. '

Right behind them walked a woman in a showy fur coat.

He saw the architect De Vlonder and his guests get into their car under the overhang. The inspection had been cancelled, that was clear. Again, the face of the man with the thin grey hair caught his attention. Now he was almost sure he knew him.

In the hall, where many of the staff had congregated, Van Straten and Hijmans were waiting for him. He brushed the snow off himself, gave the handbag to the director and told his story.

'No one understands why she took the most dangerous route.'

'And I even warned her.'

'It was impossible to stop her from going,' said Hijmans.

'If only I had sent someone with her.' Van Straten pressed her fingers together so tightly that her knuckles became white. The handbag hit against her skirt, where it left a damp spot.

'I had thought about taking her in the car,' he said.

'It would have been no use. She wanted to do everything by herself. And it was always fine, wasn't it?' Hijmans held her hands against her reddened cheeks.

'I should have watched her as usual. Why didn't I wait a moment when they called me away?'

'Don't blame yourself, Rena. I even said to her "Do go quickly".'

'Oh dear, did Frieda fall into a little hole?' The woman in the bright-green dress was suddenly behind them, her head tilted on her birdlike neck. Van Straten pushed her gently in the direction of two attendants, who took her away.

With Hijmans and a few other staff members Abels had followed the director to her office. She spread a newspaper out on a table and shook the handbag empty. Silently she looked at the pile of wet, damaged belongings, among which a silver cigarette-case and a silver photograph frame stood out. She put the cigarette-case aside. The glass in the frame was cracked, the photograph was warped, soiled, pierced by splinters. But he saw who it was.

'She didn't smoke, did she?' someone said.

'And what was she doing with that big frame in her handbag?'

'That's how she was,' said Hijmans. 'Isn't that right, Abels?'

'She had her little ways,' he said. 'It must have been something like that arithmetic of hers. She was always doing sums.' As though she could never find the solution, he had thought.

'What do we do with it?' The director was looking at a leather case which was bulging with moisture. The photographs in it were stuck together in a lump. She picked up a wallet, tapped the water off it.

'We can dry these,' said Hijmans.

'And the rest?' Van Straten hesitated. Her self-assurance had deserted her, he noticed. She seemed to be waiting for permission. With a fingertip she rubbed the photograph in the frame. The emulsion-layer dissolved and a grey spot appeared.

People nodded. She put the handbag with the other things and folded the newspaper together. 'Would you please take this away, Abels?'

When he had descended to the storage cellar he had the feeling that he was about to perform a ceremony, even though he didn't yet know what he should do. For several minutes he held the small bundle in front of him – the obliterated images of those he had known in a youth lost too soon which he, thanks to her, had been reminded of so often. Looking around he saw a shiny new dustbin standing in a corner. He walked towards it, placed the packet at the bottom and gently, almost solemnly, closed the lid.

*A*BELS SAW the motor-cycle police appear at the turn in the road. Together with a representative of the city they had escorted Frieda Borgstein on her last journey through the city. The sun gave their white helmets and white jackets a golden glow which remained until they stopped opposite the entrance to the cemetery, where birch trees cast a network of shadows. Standing next to their motor cycles, they saluted when the procession rode down the sloping path to the gate. As the last one, Abels fell in behind the group which followed the bier along the gravel path between the graves, identical stones covered with green mould, rising up thin from the frozen snow. His eyes turned towards the tops of the conifers around the graveyard, and he thought back to the conversation of the day before. First he had wanted to take no notice of the incident. But he was haunted by the face of the man on the pavement. After hesitating for a long time, he had gone to the director to ask the name of the official from the provincial department for care for the aged, in the hope that he had made a mistake. But that was not the case. A difficult telephone conversation, during which the other had shown himself very defensive, had finally resulted in an appointment. They arranged to meet in a café on Gouverneurs Square.

He was already seated at a table in the back, his pale, slightly flabby face bent forward. Not until after the coffee was brought and he had stirred it thoughtfully for a while did Hein Kessels begin to speak.

'This was bound to happen sooner or later. But that she of all people would set it in motion – call it the power of chance. If Rietmeier hadn't been in bed with flu, he would have gone to the Home as provincial representative. They asked if I would replace him. Please don't blame me for not wanting to commit myself on the telephone, but it was difficult for me – such an end, after what had already happened. I was to take them to Switzerland.'

'She told me everything.'

'Everything? She didn't know how it happened. She can't have known why it went wrong. I don't even know that myself. At that time the Resistance

96

was still poorly organized. Take our little group. We wanted to do something, but we had no experience. We provided false papers, we looked for places to hide. All that had just started then. One day I heard from someone that they smuggled people to Switzerland. I thought of Borgstein immediately. I really liked him – I knew him through my father. But you know that.'

'Were they the first ones you were to take?'

'You could say that, yes.'

'Borgstein didn't know that. He thought you had already done that escape route.'

'A misunderstanding. Three of us worked on it. When I proposed it to Borgstein, one of us had just escorted away a married couple. In our opinion the plan was watertight. I was able to prepare myself thoroughly. I was briefed by my friend who had reached Switzerland in a week and a half. I was familiar with each obstacle, the roads, the border crossings, the places to stay, the passwords – everything was in my head, not a word on paper. I thought I had everything all set.'

'With the money too. Wasn't that an enormous sum for those days?'

'It involved big expenses. I calculated it exactly for Borgstein. A family of four, that was quite a job. You could never know how long you'd be on the road. And sometimes you needed the help of people who didn't believe in charity. Others asked larger sums – five thousand per person, if not more. And then they pocketed most of it.' He lit a cigarette; his jaw trembled.

'A lot of dealing went on . . . and went wrong.'

'True. I was young, twenty-two, and as I have already said, I had no experience. We were amateurs. But I ask you, at that time how many could handle it professionally? That didn't come until later. And even then, things often went wrong.' Kessels pushed his coffee-cup aside.

How did I recognize him? Abels thought. How in this sagging man was I able to rediscover the dandyish young man with the quick movements? It must have been his eyes and his mouth and that cleft in his chin. 'Yes,' he said. 'Later, everything was much better organized. But for most people it was too late by then. They got me as well.'

'You too?' Kessels tapped the table with his lighter and stared across the café, where they were the only patrons at that moment. It seemed as though he had to gather all his strength to continue. 'That evening, 21st April 1942, I cycled to Zuid Quay – a Sunday, a quiet day, you would think.' His body shook. 'Everything was arranged. I was to bring them to an address outside the city, where they could spend the night. From there we were going to leave by car early the next morning. It wasn't even a twenty-minute walk. But that's what worried me most.'

'But they had proper papers, didn't they?'

'Yes indeed, identity cards, passports, even birth

certificates. And all four of them would carry those on their person, I had insisted on that. But in the street, in a city where so many people know you, you can't be certain of anything. I had wanted to pick them up by car. The first plan was to get as far as possible that same evening. We had one and a half hours. The Belgian border was within reach.' He shook his head, lifted his hand towards the bar and ordered a beer, waited until it was placed in front of him, greedily took a gulp.

'Why didn't you pick them up in the car?'

'It wasn't possible. That did bother me tremendously. I couldn't get the car until the next morning.'

'And then why', he continued questioning, 'didn't you wait until the next morning?'

'During the day, on Zuid Quay? That was far too risky. I don't know whether you remember the situation there. Nearly opposite the house were patrol boats of the Kriegsmarine, and in the Bastion the military police. You also saw many SS.'

'I remember.' He had watched the scene with Borgstein, the quick manoeuvres on the water, swastikas at the stern. He could still hear him say: 'When will the river be pure again?'

'I even made an attempt to get hold of another car from a former schoolmate, totally trustworthy. He also worked in the Resistance.'

'Many used to say they did.'

'I only sounded him out. Named no names. Nothing. My father needed the car himself all week. I don't know, maybe I shouldn't have done it. I've always wondered about it.'

'Didn't you find out later?'

Kessels ignored the question. He lit his fourth cigarette. 'It was dark early that evening. It was gloomy weather. It was raining. I still remember that it made me happy, as though the rain would give us extra protection.' He paused again and took a big gulp of beer. 'It doesn't speak well for me that I suspected nothing, but that's how it was. They must have followed me. From which point on I don't know. I leant my bicycle against the front of the house. It was dark, the curtains were drawn apart. I had advised them to leave them like that, to give the impression that they weren't at home. They would be standing ready in the hall, we had arranged that, then we could leave immediately. I would walk ahead with Borgstein, the others a distance behind. I looked through the small window in the door, straight into Borgstein's face. At that very moment I heard a car stop behind me.' Kessels had lowered his voice and bent forward.

Abels looked at the man's pale blue eyes, in which the whites were an unhealthy colour and revealed broken blood-vessels.

'I wanted to jump back on my bike immediately, act as if I was at the wrong address. But in the meantime Borgstein had already opened the door.'

'When he saw the car?'

'When he saw me.' Kessels straightened up, angrily crushed his cigarette-butt. 'There must have been a leak somewhere. Two men jumped out of the car, SD men.* You know the rest, I believe.'

'But how was that? Didn't they know how many people to expect?'

'That's just the thing. Clearly not. They had three for the taking in the hall, and they didn't look further. Perhaps they were content with their catch – who can say? Borgstein must have expected me to ask him where his wife was. I felt that from him. That was the worst for me. He must have assumed that they had fallen into a trap. He looked at me intently and said: "We are ready." For the rest, everything went as quick as lightning. They were thrown into the back of the car. Me they took between them. We were not allowed to exchange a word. At the SD office we were separated. I didn't see them again. That's how it happened.'

'Did you ever consider . . .'

'They questioned me endlessly. They wanted to know which sophisticated organization was behind that escape route. They assumed that as a matter of course. They couldn't imagine it was just a small group of three boys together. I didn't break down,

* SD = *Sicherheitsdienst*, the SS Security Service.

in case you think so. The other two were not caught. After that came the camps, three. I was liberated in Oraniënburg.' His heavy head had again sunk forward.

'What I don't understand is why you never visited Mrs Borgstein. Didn't you know she was still alive?'

'I knew it, but I couldn't bring myself to call on her. The first years after the war I couldn't summon the courage, and after that I pushed it out of my mind. What should I have told her?'

'What you've told me. After all, weren't you innocent?'

'Should I have said to her: "I'm sorry, I couldn't help it, I was an amateur, a bungler, I didn't expect it"? No, I didn't dare face her. And as time went by it became even harder. I wanted to forget the whole business. You can understand that, I hope?'

'Did you manage to?'

'What do you think? I went to live somewhere else, became a civil servant of the province, married, had children, grandchildren. Forget? I wish it were true. I couldn't even talk about it, until today.' Kessels loosened his tie and ran his finger inside his shirt collar.

He looked at the glass of beer which stood untouched in front of him, startled by the image that entered his mind: Frieda Borgstein, with her black coat dragging over the floor, walking away from him.

'Well yes,' Kessels said suddenly, 'I must admit, there have been periods when I didn't think about it.'

'She never had those. She always wondered why they didn't take her along at that moment and why they didn't come to pick her up later.'

Kessels tore open a packet of cigarettes. 'That proves that they knew only what I was going to do, and not how many people I was going to take.' He seemed to be in deep thought, laid down his fresh cigarette and asked, as if it hadn't entered his mind until now: 'Why was it, in fact, that she wasn't standing in the hall?'

'She had just gone upstairs to get a sweater.'

Kessels nodded vehemently. 'That's just what I mean – what chance can do to you, the absurd things which no one is willing to accept from you. I should also say that I came to the door six minutes or so earlier than we had arranged. I had cycled hard.'

'Therefore, because you came six minutes earlier. . . ?'

'Yes, but that too is not certain.' Kessels shrugged his shoulders and looked at Abels helplessly.

When Kessels walked on the narrow path between the tables towards the revolving door, Abels saw that he limped.

Abels had let the prayers at the grave go past him. He now noticed that people had started passing a small shovel to each other. It would reach him in a few minutes. He was paying attention to it, but kept thinking of what Kessels had said at the end of their conversation: 'Maybe that car was just being driven on the quay, maybe they smelt a rat because they saw me cycling so hard and therefore kept following me. Suppose I had just come to the door at the arranged time, six minutes later, who knows, those people might have passed already and it would not have happened.'

Nothing had to be proved any more, he thought, nothing explained.

Over the heads he saw a thrush alight in a conifer. It was as though it wanted to drown out the thudding of the earth on the coffin with its clear voice. Abels kept listening until he could hear only the high whistle of the bird.

P. 47

she stepped
step away
from you —

p. 65

Former neighbors looked
away —

27 — They remained young forever —

27 — Keeps adding up — trying to add it
up

47 "after every word, she took a
step away from you ..."

96 — Resistance poorly organized
April 21, 1942 —

Thrush singing —
→ conifer
Bone ruined choirs

whistler of the bird —

p. 93 — Do sums but
never find
solutions

Kaddish is said — at end
by —

Salamander —
whistle